ƒAIRY
SCHOOL
Drop-out

Over the Rainbow

Scholastic Canada Ltd.
604 King Street West, Toronto, Ontario M5V 1E1, Canada

Scholastic Inc.
557 Broadway, New York, NY 10012, USA

Scholastic Australia Pty Limited
PO Box 579, Gosford, NSW 2250, Australia

Scholastic New Zealand Limited
Private Bag 94407, Greenmount, Auckland, New Zealand

Scholastic Children's Books
Euston House, 24 Eversholt Street, London NW1 1DB, UK

Library and Archives Canada Cataloguing in Publication
Badger, Meredith
Fairy school drop-out over the rainbow / Meredith Badger ;
illustrator, Michelle Mackintosh.

ISBN 978-0-545-98977-0

I. Mackintosh, Michelle II. Title.
PZ7.B1378Fao 2009   j823'.92   C2008-905771-6

ISBN-10 0-545-98977-9

First published in Australia by Hardie Grant Egmont.
Published in Canada by Scholastic Canada Ltd., 2009

6 5 4 3 2 1   Printed in Canada   09 10 11 12 13 14

FAIRY SCHOOL Drop-out

Over the Rainbow

BY

MEREDITH BADGER

Cover and text design by Sonia Dixon Design
Illustrations by Michelle Mackintosh

Scholastic Canada Ltd.
Toronto New York London Auckland Sydney
Mexico City New Delhi Hong Kong Buenos Aires

Chapter One

Imagine this: You are walking through a park and you see a girl and an old lady hurrying along. The girl looks like a normal, average schoolgirl, except her feet are slightly on the small side and her hair is very, very shiny. Perhaps you decide that the old lady is the girl's grandmother. She looks like she's probably saying, "Come along, dear. Let's get home so your old gran can make you a batch of biscuits."

You smile, thinking, *What a lovely granny, and what a typical, ordinary girl. They must be going on a stroll together—the sort we humans go on all the time.*

Well, you were right about one thing—the old lady is the girl's grandmother. But everything else you thought was wrong. Totally, utterly wrong. For a start, there's nothing typical or ordinary about the girl. She's a fairy, and her name is Elly.

If you were a fairy expert, you might've noticed that she has exactly ten freckles and that her fingers are slightly shimmery. You wouldn't have seen her wings, though, because they were hidden beneath her clothes.

Her grandmother is a fairy too. But Elly's grandmother isn't exactly lovely.

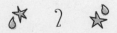 2

GRANDMOTHER KNOTTLEWEED-EVERSPRIGHTLY & ELLY

What she was actually saying to Elly as they hurried through the park was, "I don't know what your parents were thinking, sending you to a human school while they are away. It's not as if you didn't already have some very bad habits! I've left a message for your mother, telling her that I'm taking you to a *proper* fairy school. A good, strict one with no humans!"

Elly hurried along beside her grandmother. She knew better than to argue with an angry Grandmother Knottleweed-Eversprightly.

But at the same time, there were a few things worrying her. For one thing, where exactly were they going?

Elly had lived in this town all her life and she knew where all the fairy schools were. In fact, she'd already been to three of them!

Unfortunately, she'd had to leave all three of them too. Things just always seemed to go wrong for Elly at school.

Something else was on Elly's mind. *Has Grandmother even told my family which school she's sending me to?*

Elly's mum was a top inventor at Fairy Inc. She had been called away recently on a top-secret business trip. Elly's dad and baby sister Kara had gone too.

But Elly hadn't been allowed to go. The trip was so secret that her family couldn't even send Elly any wand messages to let her know where they were and what they were doing. Elly hadn't heard from them in ages.

I just hope they come back soon! Elly thought, as her grandmother dragged her along by the arm. For such a tiny lady Grandmother had a very tight grip.

She led Elly toward the centre of the local gardens.

"Um, excuse me, Grandmother," said Elly in her politest voice.

"What, Elinora?" snapped Grandmother.

"It's just that I know there aren't any fairy schools in this park," said Elly.

Grandmother stopped suddenly by the large fountain in the middle of the park. "The school I'm taking you to is not in this *park*," she retorted. "It's in Rainbowville."

Elly looked at her grandmother in surprise. "Rainbowville!" she repeated. Rainbowville was the capital of Fairydom. "I've never been."

"Well, it's about time you went," said Grandmother. "Only fairies are allowed in there. It will do you good to be separated

from all those ghastly human children."

Elly frowned, thinking about her human friends Jess and Caitlin at South Street School. Elly had only been at the school for a little while, but it was the happiest time she'd ever spent at any school. For once she was actually doing well at school. She had just started to fit in, too, when Grandmother had arrived and dragged her away!

"They're not ghastly. Most of them are really nice," Elly said crossly. "Much nicer than a lot of fairies I know," she added under her breath. "Like Gabi Cruddleperry, for instance."

Gabilotta Cruddleperry had been at Elly's last fairy school—Mossy Blossom Academy. She and Elly had been enemies ever since Elly had accidentally given her a big moustache

7

on their first day of school. Gabi had been trying to get even with Elly ever since.

"What?" asked Grandmother sharply.

"Nothing!" Elly replied hastily. "I was just wondering—how do we get to Rainbowville?"

Grandmother looked annoyed. "Over the rainbow, of course!" she said. "You should know all about the Rainbow Portal from reading the Fairy Code."

Elly kept quiet. The Fairy Code was a huge rule book that schoolfairies were supposed to read every day. Whenever Elly tried to read it, however, she fell asleep! But there was no way she could tell Grandmother that. Especially as some Knottleweed-Eversprightly ancestor had helped write it.

"We need to catch ourselves a rainbow," said Grandmother, producing a large, multi-

coloured umbrella from somewhere in her coat.

Elly looked up at the clear blue sky. "I don't think it's going to rain," she said doubtfully. "And besides, just as you get close to a rainbow, it vanishes!"

Grandmother unfurled the umbrella. "It's not a matter of finding the end of the rainbow," she explained condescendingly. "It's about getting the rainbow to come to you."

Elly had to try very hard not to giggle. Everyone knew that rainbows didn't come to you when you called!

But then Grandmother held the umbrella up and the most extraordinary thing happened. Droplets of water began rising

out of the fountain and floating toward the umbrella. Before long, a fine mist hung in the air. Then a rainbow appeared in the centre of the mist, arching up into the sky.

"Wow!" gasped Elly.

The rainbow was very bright, and the colours seemed to pulse and shimmer. As Elly watched, the rainbow grew bigger and stronger, stretching up into the sky.

"Come here," instructed Grandmother. She grabbed Elly and jumped onto the rainbow.

Then Elly found herself hurtling up the rainbow. *I feel like I'm on a giant roller coaster,* giggled Elly to herself, as she whooshed higher and higher. *I wish I could do this on my skateboard!*

The rainbow was smooth and slightly

spongy to sit on, but completely dry. Elly gripped the rainbow's sides to steady herself.

Down below, the town got smaller and smaller until Elly could hardly see it at all.

With a little bounce, Elly and her grandmother arrived at the top of the rainbow. Looking down, Elly saw something amazing. On one side of the rainbow was the town she'd grown up in. And on the other side was a vast, magical-looking city, twinkling and gleaming in the sunlight.

Rainbowville! thought Elly excitedly.

"Hold on very tight, Elinora!" called Grandmother, as they began zooming down the other side. "We're almost there."

Chapter Two

The closer Elly and Grandmother got to the ground, the clearer the sights and sounds of Rainbowville became. Tall buildings pointed toward the sky, glimmering and catching the light like they were made from crystal. Around the buildings were beautiful parks, filled with brightly coloured trees and flowers. And everywhere Elly looked, there were hundreds of fairies!

Elly's parents sometimes talked about

Rainbowville, but Elly had never paid much attention. She'd never been all that interested in it. She'd vaguely pictured Rainbowville as a storybook kind of place, with lots of old-fashioned cottages and cobbled streets.

But from up on the rainbow, Rainbowville actually looked very modern. All the fairies seemed to be wearing very trendy clothes. There wasn't a tutu in sight!

Some of them weren't even flying, but riding on skateboards—in mid-air!

I wish I had my skateboard, thought Elly wistfully. Her skateboard was her favourite way to get around, but now it was back on the other side of the rainbow.

And I wish Jess were here. Jess was Elly's human friend. She lived next door to Elly's family in Raspberry Drive, and was always

interested in Elly's fairy gadgets. Elly knew Jess would be fascinated by Rainbowville.

Saphie would like it here too, I bet! thought Elly. Saphie was Elly's best fairy friend at Mossy Blossom. Unfortunately, just like Jess, Saphie was now far away on the other side of the rainbow.

Suddenly, Elly really missed her friends. Coming to Rainbowville would have been a great adventure if her friends were with her too. But being here with Grandmother wouldn't be nearly as much fun.

"Get ready to land, Elinora!" called Grandmother suddenly.

The ground seemed to be heading toward them at an alarming rate. *We're going to crash!* Elly thought.

But just as they reached the end of the

rainbow, they slowed down and plopped gently into a large, golden pot full of comfy cushions. A rainbow-coloured mist swirled around them.

"Is this the pot of gold at the end of the rainbow that humans are always talking about?" asked Elly.

"Indeed," replied Grandmother, tucking the rainbow umbrella under her arm and flying neatly out of the pot. "But as usual, the humans got it completely wrong. As you can see, it's really a pot *made* of gold, rather than a pot *full of* gold."

Elly caught sight of a small pipe sticking up through the base of the pot. The rainbow-coloured mist seemed to be coming out of it.

"Grandmother, where does that pipe lead to?" Elly asked curiously.

Grandmother frowned. "You ask too many questions, Elinora," she said. "But if you *must* know, it leads to the Rainbow Laboratory. That's where the rainbow is made."

RAINBOW FACTS

The rainbow is a bridge between the human and fairy realms.

At the end is a pot made of gold, rather than a pot full of gold.

The rainbow-coloured mist is made at the Rainbow Laboratory.

"Really!" said Elly. "Can we have a look?"

"Certainly not!" said Grandmother briskly. "The Rainbow Laboratory is top secret. Unlicensed fairies are not allowed in. Now come along and stop dawdling."

Elly untucked her wings and flew out of the pot, landing beside her grandmother. *I wish I could explore Rainbowville by myself,* thought Elly longingly.

Then she heard a strange, whirring noise above her. Looking up, she saw what seemed to be a huge pen, scribbling in the sky. Large cloud-like letters were forming as it wrote.

Elly's mouth fell open when she saw what the letters spelled. "Grandmother!" she gasped. "That giant pen wrote our names in the sky!"

"It's not a giant pen, Elinora," Grandmother

corrected. "It's a Cloud Writer. It writes the name of anyone who enters or leaves Rainbowville. It's to make sure no humans wander through accidentally. And it's also a way of stopping young fairies from sneaking out. Unlicensed fairies like yourself aren't

it knows who you are!

sky scanner buttons

runs on steam

CLOUD WRITER

allowed out of Rainbowville unsupervised."

Elly gulped. That meant she was trapped here! "How does it know who I am?" she asked.

"Because of the Sky Scanner, of course," said Grandmother crossly, as if Elly should know all about it. "It watches to see whoever is entering or exiting Rainbowville. Then it scans them to discover their identity. The visitor's name is sent straight to the Cloud Writer."

Elly watched as a breeze blew and the cloud writing disappeared. Then she gave an enormous yawn. "Excuse me, Grandmother," she said hurriedly, because Grandmother thought yawning was very rude. "Suddenly I feel incredibly tired."

"Well, of course you do!" Grandmother replied. "Human time and fairy time is different. One fairy day equals a whole week

in human time." Then she grasped Elly firmly by the wrist. "Come along. The sooner we get you settled into your new school the better."

"Is it far?" asked Elly, feeling nervous.

"Not far at all," said Grandmother. "Turn around."

Elly turned. Behind them was a vast building, glowing and twinkling like a jewel. It changed colours too. One moment it was pink, then it was turquoise, then silvery-blue.

"It's so beautiful!" said Elly, surprised. She hadn't thought the school would look like *this*.

"Of course!" said Grandmother. "It's the Rainbow Academy for Fairies, after all—the finest and most prestigious school in all of Rainbowville. I went there and so did your mother. And now you are going there. I hope you will add further glory to the Knottleweed-Eversprightly name."

"Er, well . . . I'll do my best," said Elly uncertainly. She didn't exactly have a great record of doing well at fairy schools.

"I certainly hope you will," replied Grandmother crisply, turning toward the school's arched front gates.

Elly looked up. The sky was getting dark. All around her, fairies were hurrying home for the night. "Excuse me, Grandmother, but isn't it a bit late to be going to school today? Everyone will have gone by now."

"I doubt that very much," Grandmother retorted. "The Rainbow Academy is a boarding school, after all."

Elly stared at her grandmother in horror. "A *boarding* school!" she exclaimed. "You

didn't tell me that!"

Grandmother turned to Elly and raised an eyebrow. "You don't have to go there if you don't want to, Elinora," she said.

"Really?" asked Elly suspiciously.

"Of course not," said Grandmother. "You can always be tutored privately by me. Classes would run from 7 a.m. to 7 p.m. every day, with a 15-minute break for lunch. Every month or so you could have a half-day off."

Elly gulped and began flying toward the Rainbow Academy. "Come on, Grandmother," she said quickly. "We'd better get there as soon as we can!"

I'm sure Mum and Dad will come and get me before too long, Elly told herself. *I just hope that it's sooner rather than later . . .*

Chapter Three

Soon Elly and Grandmother were flying through the rainbow-shaped gates of the Academy and up to the front door. Up close, the whole building was slightly see-through, as if it were made entirely of crystals. Elly could see figures moving around inside.

Grandmother rang the doorbell and a moment later the door was opened by an elegant fairy with grey wings and a tower of white hair piled high on her head.

At first the fairy looked stern, but her face broke into smiles when she saw Grandmother. "Fifibella Knottleweed-Eversprightly!" she exclaimed. "How lovely to see you!"

"Emerelda Fernyfrond, my dear," replied Grandmother warmly. "You look wonderful!"

Elly was surprised. Grandmother hardly ever smiled.

"Madame Fernyfrond and I were students together at the Academy, Elly," explained Grandmother. "Now she's the headfairy here."

Grandmother turned back to Madame Fernyfrond. "This is my granddaughter, Elinora. I'm hoping you have room for her, Emmy."

Madame Fernyfrond studied Elly, and Elly suddenly felt very self-conscious. She remembered the smudge of ink on her nose, and her messy hair. If Madame Fernyfrond was anything like Grandmother, these were things she would disapprove of highly.

But Madame Fernyfrond smiled. "There's always room for a Knottleweed-Eversprightly at Rainbow Academy. You do have a big reputation to live up to here, Elinora," she said, patting Elly's shoulder. "Your mother finished top of her class. And your grandmother is one of our most famous graduates."

"Elinora has picked up some very bad habits from humans," said Grandmother disapprovingly. "I'm hoping you can help turn her into a proper fairy."

"I understand completely," nodded Madame Fernyfrond. "My own granddaughter has just started here as well. I suspect she's also spent far too long around humans, and has started to go quite wild! She's quite badly behaved and dreadfully rude. Those human children are such a bad influence."

"Exactly," agreed Grandmother. "Which is why I knew Rainbow Academy would be the perfect place to put Elinora on the right path."

"I will certainly do my best," said Madame Fernyfrond. "Elinora can share a dormitory with my granddaughter. That way I can keep a special eye on the two of them."

Elly's heart sank. She didn't want to share with Madame Fernyfrond's rude, badly behaved granddaughter. And she hated the idea of having a "special eye" kept on her.

But Elly knew that if she complained, she would end up being privately tutored by Grandmother!

"Come inside," said Madame Fernyfrond. "I'll show you to your dormitory. My granddaughter can give you a tour of the school. Are you coming, Fifi?"

"Thank you Emmy, but I must fly," said Grandmother. Then she looked sternly at Elly. "Elinora, I hope you will make the most of this wonderful opportunity. Make sure you do everything Madame Fernyfrond tells you."

"Yes, Grandmother," replied Elly politely.

It wasn't until after Grandmother had

flown away that Elly noticed something lying on the ground. It was the rainbow umbrella!

Grandmother must have dropped it, thought Elly, picking it up.

She put the umbrella in her backpack. *I'll give it back to Grandmother next time I see her,* she decided.

"Here, Elinora. Take this," said Madame Fernyfrond, handing her what looked like an ordinary ruler.

"It's the Rainbow Academy Rule Ruler. New pupils must carry it around until they learn all the school rules. You should start listening straight away, Elinora, as there are quite a few."

"Rule number one," said the Rule Ruler in a prim little voice. "You must learn all the rules by heart."

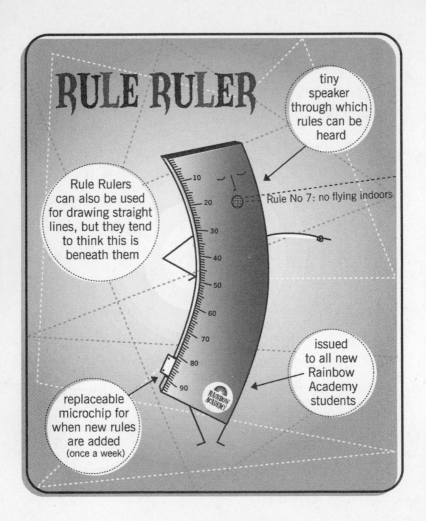

Madame Fernyfrond turned and headed down the corridor. "Come along!" she called.

Elly had to fly to catch up with her.

"Rule number seven," said the Ruler. "No flying indoors."

Hastily, Elly dropped to the ground. But the floor was so slippery that she fell over.

"Rule number 53," said the Ruler instantly. "No falling over."

Elly stood up, sighing.

"Rule number 849," said the Ruler. "No sighing."

Elly glared at the Ruler. "You're just making these rules up as we go along!" she muttered. "I wonder if I could just accidentally-on-purpose lose you somewhere?"

"Rule number four," said the Ruler quickly. "No losing the Rule Ruler."

Elly headed off after Madame Fernyfrond again, who was by now a long way ahead. Immediately, she fell over again.

"Rule number 132—no falling over," said the Ruler.

Elly frowned. "You've already said that one! With a different number!"

"Rule number 20," said the Ruler bossily. "No arguing with the Rule Ruler."

Madame Fernyfrond turned around. "What *are* you doing, Elinora?"

"I can't seem to walk along these floors, Madame Fernyfrond," Elly explained.

"Well, it's no wonder!" said Madame, examining Elly's shoes. "Those clodhopping human shoes are not suitable for these floors."

"Rule number 597," chimed in the Ruler. "No human shoes."

From a pocket in her gown, Madame Fernyfrond produced a pair of blue slippers. "Put these on," said Madame Fernyfrond, "and then flutter your wings just slightly as you glide along."

After that, Elly found it much easier to move across the slippery corridors, although it took a while to get the hang of it. If she beat her wings even slightly too hard, she ended up sliding into the walls!

Elly and Madame Fernyfrond passed some students who gave Elly curious looks. Elly looked back at them just as curiously. They were all dressed in knee-length deep-blue tunics that buttoned up over the shoulders, paired with rainbow-striped stockings.

That must be the uniform here, thought Elly, relieved. All of the fairy schools she'd been to before had very traditional fairy outfits, complete with scratchy, itchy tutus. Elly hated them! At least these uniforms looked comfortable. Elly hummed to herself, feeling a little happier.

But the Ruler interrupted her. "Rule number 175—no humming."

Elly sighed, remembering the noise and bustle of South Street School. Even at Mossy Blossom Academy they'd been allowed to make noise at lunchtime. She and Saphie had always made the biggest racket of all!

Elly's home was very noisy too. Baby Kara was always making things fall over with a

bang. Her mum was always crashing about in her inventing studio. And her dad liked singing duets with their musical bathtub at the top of his voice.

Suddenly, Elly felt so homesick that it was all she could do not to burst into tears.

Finally, Madame Fernyfrond came to a stop outside a bright blue door with a number five on it. "This is your dormitory," she said, rapping sharply on the door.

"Come in!" called a friendly voice.

Inside were four beds hanging from the ceiling like swings. The walls, the curtains and the rug were blue. The beds were covered in blue bedspreads. Even the light bulb was blue. Lying on one of the beds, reading a book, was a small, pretty fairy.

"Elinora, this is my granddaughter . . ."

Madame Fernyfrond started to say.

But Elly needed no introduction. She had already flown up to the bed and flung her arms around the surprised fairy.

"Saphie!" cried Elly. "You have no idea how happy I am to see you!"

Chapter Four

Saphie was equally happy to see Elly. "But what are you doing here?" she asked.

"It was Grandmother's idea," explained Elly.

Saphie smiled. "Same here!" she said. "My family came for a visit to Rainbowville, and Grandma Fernyfrond convinced them that I should attend the Rainbow Academy."

"And you've already improved vastly in the short time you've been here," said

Madame Fernyfrond.

Elly felt like giggling. Saphie was the most perfect fairy she knew. She always got 100% in her spelling tests and she knew how to do all kinds of extra-tricky stunt flying. And she never forgot to recharge her wand, like Elly did. How could Saphie *possibly* improve?

"Thank you, Grandma," said Saphie politely, without looking even slightly annoyed. Saphie was perfect when it came to manners too!

Just then, a bell chimed.

"Ah, dinnertime!" said Madame Fernyfrond. "Sapphire, please take Elinora down to the dining hall, and then help get her set up." Madame glided out the door.

Elly grinned at Saphie. "It's just like we're back at Mossy Blossom together!"

Saphie pulled a face. "More than you realize, unfortunately. There's another student here from Mossy Blossom, as it happens."

"Who?" asked Elly curiously.

"Who would be the last fairy in the whole of the Fairy Realm that you would want to share a dormitory with?"

Elly looked at Saphie in horror. "No way!"

Saphie nodded. "Gabi Cruddleperry!"

"Oh no!" said Elly. "Please tell me that she's nicer than she used to be, at least?"

Saphie shook her head. "Sorry," she said. "She's worse than ever. She's decided that she's the best fairy here and she's always doing magic when she's not supposed to. And somehow she keeps getting away with it. Yesterday, she put a dizzy spell on Evie Glitterwings. Every time Evie tried to stand up, she'd just fall over again. Gabi thought it was really funny."

"That's terrible!" groaned Elly.

"It gets worse," said Saphie. "The fourth fairy in our room is Gabi's cousin, Nadia."

"You mean we're sharing with *two* Cruddleperrys?" said Elly in disbelief.

Saphie nodded. "Afraid so," she said, giving Elly's hand a squeeze. "Which is why I'm so extra-specially pleased to see you. It's been terrible dealing with them on my own.

Gabi is still really cross with you, but because you're not around she picks on me instead! Nadia is just as bad. Last night they changed my toothbrush into a big slug. And last week they turned my sheets into cheese while I was asleep. When I woke up they'd melted all over me!"

Elly frowned. "That won't happen again, ever!" she promised. "No one melts cheese on my friends while I'm around."

Saphie laughed and gave her friend a huge hug. "I'm so glad you're here!" she said. "Now, we'd better hurry."

"Rule number 348," the Ruler piped up. "No being late for dinner."

Saphie leapt down from the bed, landing gracefully on the ground.

Elly did the same, but not nearly so gracefully.

"Let's go," said Saphie. "And leave that annoying Ruler in your drawer!"

"*Great* idea!" laughed Elly.

"Rule number nine! No leaving the Ruler behind!" shrieked the Ruler, as Elly and Saphie headed out the door.

Cooking smells wafted up the corridor as Saphie and Elly neared the dining room.

"What's for dinner tonight?" asked Elly, sniffing hungrily.

"Well, today is blue day," said Saphie, "so it's probably blue soup, followed by blue

stew and blueberry pie to finish."

"*Blue* day?" repeated Elly.

"Every day here is dedicated to a different colour of the rainbow," explained Saphie as they entered the dining hall. "Today's colour is blue, so we wear blue uniforms and eat blue food. Tomorrow is indigo, so we have to wear our indigo uniforms and eat indigo food."

Elly giggled. "That's the craziest thing I've ever heard!"

"I thought so too, at first," agreed Saphie. "But I'm used to it now. And the food is actually pretty tasty."

Elly wasn't sure she believed Saphie when she was handed a big bowl of blue soup. It smelled OK. But it looked like paint!

"Don't worry, it's nice," whispered Saphie. "They make it out of special blue tomatoes. It tastes just like red tomato soup, I promise."

Elly took a little sip with her eyes closed. To her surprise, Saphie was right! It tasted exactly like tomato soup.

Then Elly tried another mouthful, with her eyes open. But for some reason now it tasted, well, *blue*!

"I feel like I'm sleep-eating!" Elly giggled to Saphie, closing her eyes again.

After dinner, Saphie took Elly on a quick tour of the school.

"That's the Flight Simulator room, where we do Extreme Flying," Saphie said, as they glided past a series of blue doors. "This next room is where we do Human Studies. It's set up to look like a human classroom. And that,"

added Saphie, pointing to a heavy-looking door, "is the library. Hardly anyone goes there because they all listen to wandbooks instead. I like it, though. It's a good place to escape from the Cruddleperrys!"

Next to the library door was a shining silver gate, padlocked shut. Behind it was a dark, narrow set of stairs leading downwards.

Elly stopped and stared into the gloom. "What's down there?"

"The Rainbow Laboratory," replied Saphie. "It's located right below the school."

"The Rainbow Laboratory," echoed Elly, remembering what Grandmother had told her. "Isn't that where the rainbow is made?"

Saphie nodded. "Yes. It's also where the main Sky Scanner is kept," she said. "It's an incredibly important place."

"I'd love to have a look in there," said Elly longingly.

"Forget it," sighed Saphie. "Only a few of the very top students in the very top class are ever allowed in."

Just then, a bell rang.

"That's the bedtime bell," said Saphie. "Come on. We'd better go. I can just hear that Rule Ruler now. *Rule number eleventy-million. No ignoring the bedtime bell!*"

Elly took one last look at the stairs. She knew she'd probably never get into the Rainbow Laboratory. But that didn't stop her from really wanting to!

chapter Five

When Elly and Saphie arrived back at their dormitory, they were shocked by what they saw. The room was in total chaos! Papers and books were scattered everywhere. The bedspreads were lying in a jumbled heap on the floor. And huddled up together on one of the beds were two girls, looking very scared.

Elly recognized Gabi Cruddleperry. *The other girl must be her cousin Nadia,* she realized. *I'd know a Cruddleperry anywhere!*

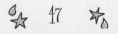

"What's going on?" asked Saphie.

Gabi pointed a trembling finger toward the cupboard. "There's a ghost in there," she whimpered. "We managed to trap it, but who knows how long that door will hold?"

Sure enough, there was a furious banging sound coming from the cupboard, like something was hurling itself against the door. And the closer Elly got to the door, the more furious the banging became.

"It's probably just a bird that got stuck in here," said Elly, trying to sound brave.

Gabi shook her head. "It isn't a bird. It's an enormous blue ghost," she insisted.

"Well, there's only one way to find out for sure!" said Elly.

With her heart racing, she flung the door open. Immediately, something flew out of

the cupboard, covered in a blue sheet. Then it started flying crazily around the room, bumping into things as it went.

"See! It's a ghost!" shrieked Nadia.

Elly jumped up, grabbed the sheet as the thing flew past and yanked hard. The sheet fell off to reveal a small package, covered in stamps.

Once the sheet was off, the parcel stopped flying madly and darted straight into Elly's hands.

Saphie laughed. "It's just an express parcel with homing stamps on it. Looks like someone's sent you something, Elly! It must've got tangled up with the laundry when it was trying to find you."

Gabi and Nadia stopped looking scared and started looking annoyed instead.

"See, Nadia? I told you Elly was trouble," said Gabi crossly, jumping down from her bed. "Let's go and get some hot chocolate from the kitchen."

Then Nadia glared at Elly. "When we come back this room better be tidy."

Elly rolled her eyes at Saphie as the Cruddleperrys stalked out.

"See what I mean?" said Saphie, shaking her head. "Worse than ever."

But Elly grinned. "Forget about them," she said, plonking herself down on the floor. "Let's open my parcel."

Inside the parcel was a small, heart-shaped pendant on a chain. A butterfly-shaped card fluttered out, which Elly carefully caught.

She recognized her mum's handwriting straight away—it was always hard to read.

Darling Elly,

Here is a Heart Tracker pendant to remind you that we are thinking of you constantly. When someone who really cares about you is nearby, it glows.

Love from Mum, Dad and Kara.

Elly felt tears in her eyes as she slipped the pendant on. "I miss them so much!" she said.

Saphie nodded. "I miss my family too," she admitted. "But at least we can look after each other now." As Saphie spoke, the heart on the pendant glowed with a soft, pink light.

Elly gave Saphie's hand a grateful squeeze. She was so lucky to have a friend like her!

"Come on," Elly said, jumping up and brushing her tears away. "We better get this room tidy. If I have to listen to any more Cruddleperry complaints tonight my ears will pop!"

The next morning, Elly woke to discover that everything in their room had changed from blue to a deep purple colour. Even the door!

"It's all done with colour timers," explained Saphie, as they put on their indigo uniforms. "It just changes automatically overnight."

The indigo breakfast was raisin toast with blackberry jam, which tasted deliciously purple. But Elly's enjoyment was spoiled somewhat by the Cruddleperrys, who sat at a nearby table staring at Elly and muttering to each other.

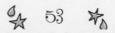

"I've got a very bad feeling about those Cruddleperrys," Elly whispered to Saphie.

"Same here," agreed Saphie. "They're definitely up to something. But what?"

After breakfast, Saphie took Elly to the Flight Simulator room for their first class, Extreme Flying.

"Miss Blippy is nice," whispered Saphie, "but she likes us to get things right the first time."

Great, thought Elly gloomily.

Miss Blippy approached Elly. "You must be Elly!" she said, smiling broadly. "I went to school with your mother. She was a brilliant flyer. I daresay you are too!"

Elly sighed. It was really hard trying to live up to the Knottleweed-Eversprightly name. Her relatives were all such high achievers.

Everyone expected Elly to be the same.

"No, I'm not, Miss Blippy," said Elly earnestly.

But Miss Blippy just laughed. "And modest, too, just like your mum! How about you start us off today?"

She handed Elly two silver things that looked like bangles. "These are turbo boosters," she explained. "They make you fly much faster. Normally I wouldn't give them to a new student, but as you're a Knottleweed-Eversprightly I'm sure there's nothing to worry about."

"I wouldn't be so sure, Miss Blippy," said Elly nervously. "In fact, maybe I should just watch this time?"

"Nonsense!" said Miss Blippy. "Now, hold on everyone!" Then, pressing a button on her wand, she launched the Flight Simulator.

Immediately, the room darkened and a gale began to howl. Lightning flashed overhead and thunder made the floor tremble and shake. A line of trees sprang up along the walls, bending backwards and forwards as they were lashed by the furious storm.

"Up you go, Elly!" shouted Miss Blippy.

Elly knew she had no choice. She clipped the turbo boosters around her ankles and immediately they roared to life. Elly found herself being dragged into the air—feet first! Somehow, she struggled back upright.

"Float around the room!" called Miss Blippy.

Float? thought Elly. She was heading into a massive storm—practically a *cyclone*—and Miss Blippy was telling her to *float*?

OK, don't panic, Elly told herself. *You've*

done Extreme Flying before. Just remember the three rules in the Fairy Code.

Generally, Elly never remembered things like this. But, luckily, today she did.

1. Keep your wings at a 90 degree angle to your body.

2. Press your arms as close to your body as possible and keep your toes pointed.

3. Tuck your chin in tightly.

Or was it stick your chin out? There was no time to decide. Elly could feel herself starting to roll over. *I'll try sticking out my chin and see what happens*, she thought desperately.

So Elly did, and for a moment her flying seemed under control. She found a gentle upward current and started drifting out of the storm.

Then from nowhere, a cold downward current flipped her upside down like a pancake. Down on the ground she could hear her classmates giggling, especially Gabi and Nadia.

"I'm stuck, Miss Blippy," Elly called helplessly, zooming around upside down.

"Turn your turbo boosters off then and come back down," said Miss Blippy.

Elly reached down and fumbled with the boosters. But instead of turning off, the boosters suddenly roared even louder than before. And Elly found herself being dragged across the room by her ankles.

"You've switched them into Overdrive!" Miss Blippy yelled. "Switch off the boosters immediately before you crash!"

But there was no way Elly could reach the boosters now. She was feeling very dizzy. She was also starting to worry.

I'm going to be flying around up here forever! she thought anxiously.

As she spun around, she caught a glimpse of her classmates' faces. No one was laughing anymore. Not even Gabi and Nadia.

turbo-booster overdrive

Chapter Six

"Hang in there, Elly!" called Miss Blippy, pushing a button on her wand.

The Flight Simulation storm flickered and spluttered, then finally vanished. Instantly, the wind died down. Miss Blippy pointed the wand at Elly's feet as she zoomed around the room, still dangling upside down.

"I'm taking over the controls of the turbo boosters, Elly," she said. "I'll have you down in a moment."

Elly felt herself moving wherever Miss Blippy's wand went. Gently, the teacher guided her back down until she landed with a gentle thud on the ground.

Now that everyone could see she was OK, the class started giggling again. Only Saphie and Evie Glitterwings didn't laugh.

"Typical!" Elly heard Gabi snigger. "Once a fairy school drop-out, *always* a fairy school drop-out."

"What kind of fairy doesn't even know how to fly properly?" added Nadia nastily.

"Oh, and I suppose you two were *perfect* with the turbo boosters straight away?" retorted Elly.

Saphie helped Elly up. "Actually," she said, "the first time Gabi and Nadia used the boosters they crashed right into each other."

GABI

NADIA

Some of the other fairies started to laugh. "That's right!" chuckled Evie. "You should've heard the way they carried on about it too. They weren't nearly as brave as you, Elly."

"The next class is Human Studies," said Saphie encouragingly, as the bell rang. "You'll be great at that. And Miss Riverella, the teacher, is really nice."

Gabi snorted. "Elly will be just as bad in

Human Studies as she is in everything else," she said. "I bet it won't be long before she's thrown out of the Rainbow Academy."

"Yeah," sneered Nadia. "In fact, we're going to make *sure* of it!"

"I will do just fine in Human Studies," said Elly, sounding more confident than she felt. "I've been to a human school, after all."

All the same, she couldn't help feeling nervous as she and Saphie headed to the next class. What exactly did Nadia have planned?

When they arrived at the Human Studies classroom, Miss Riverella wasn't there.

Instead, Madame Fernyfrond was standing at the front of the class. "I've decided to teach this class myself," she announced, "so I can keep an eye on my granddaughter and her little friend."

"But Grandma," said Saphie doubtfully, "you haven't met a human in years."

"That doesn't matter," Madame Fernyfrond said dismissively. "I know what they're like."

Elly glanced around the classroom. It looked exactly like her classroom at South Street School! Elly half-expected Jess and her other human friends to walk in.

Madame Fernyfrond saw Elly looking around. "I know what you're thinking, Elly," she said. "This room looks *nothing* like a real human classroom." She pressed a button on her wand, and all the tables and chairs turned by themselves to face the back of the room.

"Now, everyone, stand on your heads on the seats," she instructed. "Human students sit like this in class to help the circulation of blood through their brains."

Elly stared at the headfairy in surprise. *Is this a joke?*

"Of course, in some human schools, the students sit in bathtubs," Madame Fernyfrond added. "They believe this helps them absorb what they are taught."

"Excuse me, Madame Fernyfrond," said Elly, putting her wand in the air. "Humans don't really have lessons in bathtubs. And they don't do headstands in their seats!"

Madame frowned. "Of course they do!"

Elly was about to say that she had been to a human school, and was positive that no one sat in bathtubs, when Saphie caught her eye and shook her head. Then, using the mini-Cloud Writer function on her wand, she scribbled a quick message in the air for Elly.

Just agree with her!

 65

"Another interesting fact about human schools is that the pupils keep their eyes shut throughout the entire day," said Madame Fernyfrond. "Isn't that right, Elly?"

Elly tried very hard not to laugh. "Yes, Madame," she said. Then, winking at Saphie, she added, "and they hop backwards home from school every afternoon."

"Really?" said Madame Fernyfrond. "How very interesting!"

Elly leaned over to Saphie. "I don't think Madame Fernyfrond has *ever* been to a human school," she whispered.

"She has crazy ideas about humans, doesn't she? Just like humans do about fairies," grinned Saphie.

Madame Fernyfrond clapped her hands. "Who can tell me about the Human Database?"

Nadia Cruddleperry put up her wand. "It's the information that fairies have collected about humans," she said. "It's the only way to tell if a human needs a wish granted."

There's another way of knowing, thought Elly. *You can talk to them!* She had granted a wish for Jess before, and she hadn't needed to use the Human Database at all.

I wonder how Jess is going? Elly thought suddenly. It was weird to think that a week

67

had already passed by for Jess since Elly left—even though Elly had only been in Rainbowville for a day. *Lots of things could have happened in a week, and I don't know anything about them!*

Madame Fernyfrond pointed her wand at a blank wall. Instantly, a beam of light shot out and a glowing projection screen appeared.

"I will demonstrate how the Human Database works," she announced. "Now, can anyone suggest a human name that I might search for on the Database? Just make one up.

Remember, human names are sometimes quite ridiculous."

Elly sat up straight. *This is my way of finding out how Jess is,* she thought excitedly. "Jess," said Elly quickly. "Jess Chester."

"That's a particularly silly name!" laughed Madame Fernyfrond. "I doubt even a human would be called something so strange. But let's try it anyway."

Then, on the tiny keyboard on her wand, she began typing. Instantly, the screen filled with writing. Elly leaned forward eagerly. But then she sat back again, disappointed. The writing wasn't like anything she'd seen before. It was all squiggly and swirly.

"The Database has recently been converted into a special coded language," explained Madame. "This is to stop humans from accidentally discovering it on their *internut*."

Elly put her wand in the air. "Madame Fernyfrond," she said, "can you read the code? Can you tell us what it's saying about Jess?"

"Of course I can!" replied Madame Fernyfrond, a little haughtily. Then she peered at the projection for a very long time. "Jess Chester is not quite herself at the moment, according to the Database," said Madame Fernyfrond eventually.

Elly bit her lip. That didn't sound good! "Does it say anything else?" she asked.

Madame Fernyfrond squinted at the projection again. "Oh, no wonder she's not feeling very well!" she said, after a moment. "It says quite clearly that Jess is currently being crushed."

"Crushed!" repeated Elly, shocked.

Madame nodded. "Yes. And according to this, she's finding it *most* uncomfortable."

Elly stared at Madame in horror.

"Look at Elly's stupid expression," Gabi sneered to Nadia. "A proper fairy would never pull a face like that."

But Elly barely heard her. Her mind was racing. What was crushing poor Jess? Perhaps Madame had read the code incorrectly. Her lesson about human classrooms hadn't been exactly accurate, after all. But then, maybe she was right! Elly couldn't stand the thought of sitting around doing nothing if Jess was in trouble.

I've got to get out of Rainbowville as quickly as possible, thought Elly, *and find out what's going on with Jess!*

Chapter Seven

The next class was Wish Fulfillment. Elly knew she should concentrate, especially as Madame Fernyfrond was in charge again. But her mind kept wandering back to Jess.

I have to see her, thought Elly. *But how?*

"Elly!" called Madame suddenly. "Can you give us an example of a wish, please?"

"I wish I could get out of Rainbowville," replied Elly, without thinking.

Madame laughed. "Completely impossible!"

"Rule number 331," piped up Elly's Ruler. "Unlicensed fairies are not allowed out of Rainbowville."

"Exactly," agreed Madame. "If you tried to sneak out unchaperoned, the Cloud Writer would write your name in red in the sky and you'd be caught immediately."

"You'd never even make it out of the school," added Gabi. "All the gates, doors and windows have Fairy Trackers on them. If you so much as touch them, the alarm goes off."

"The only way you're leaving here," hissed Nadia, "is when you get expelled!"

Elly pulled a face at the Cruddleperrys, but inside her hopes were fading. *Are they right?* she wondered. *Is it really impossible to leave this place?*

"Elly's wish was impossible," said Madame Fernyfrond. "Gabi, can *you* give an example?"

Gabi shot a mischievous look at Elly. "Well," she said, "someone might wish for a new hairstyle."

"Excellent suggestion," said Madame Fernyfrond approvingly. "And what would you do to grant that?"

"I would do a hair realignment with my wand," replied Gabi sweetly.

"Correct," said Madame Fernyfrond, turning to write something on the board.

The moment Madame Fernyfrond's back was turned, Gabi pointed her wand at Elly's

head. Instantly, Elly had the odd sensation that her hair was moving by itself, wriggling and squirming like it had come to life.

"What's going on?" Elly whispered to Saphie nervously.

Saphie stared at her hair, looking shocked.

"What? What?" asked Elly.

Saphie pointed to Elly's reflection in the classroom window. Elly could hardly believe what she saw.

Her hair was busily wrapping itself into hundreds of tiny little braids! Then the finished braids were standing up like stalks all over her head.

Madame turned and stared at Elly in astonishment. "Elly! *What* have you done to your hair?"

"It wasn't me, Madame," protested Elly.

"No excuses, Elinora," Madame snapped. "Your grandmother warned me about your odd behaviour, and I can see she wasn't exaggerating."

Madame looked around the room. "What about you, Nadia? Can you suggest a wish?"

"You might wish for a brand new outfit," said Nadia innocently. She had her wand pointed at Elly under the desk.

"Don't!" Elly yelped, but it was too late. She suddenly felt very cold. She peered down.

"Oh, *no*!" she groaned, her face blushing bright red as everyone started laughing. She was now wearing a bathing suit! There were even flippers on her feet.

Madame Fernyfrond glared. "Elinora!" she said crossly. "Are you familiar with rule number 40?"

"Rule number 40," recited the Ruler. "No unsupervised spells by unlicensed fairies!"

"Can't you get *expelled* for that kind of thing, Madame?" asked Nadia.

"It's possible," said Madame darkly.

Then Gabi put up her wand. "I just thought of another wish, Madame Fernyfrond," she said brightly. "You might wish you were somewhere else."

"No!" cried Elly, and quickly tried to perform a blocking spell with her wand. But it didn't work. A second later Elly found herself squashed into a small, dark room.

Where am I? she wondered, groping

around for a door. Suddenly, something jabbed her very sharply in the back. Elly was flung forward through a doorway and then landed with a splat on the floor.

Elly lifted her head up. She was back in her classroom, and everyone was staring at her in amazement, except for the Cruddleperrys, who looked like they were about to explode from trying not to laugh.

"It's no good hiding in the broom closet, Elinora," frowned Madame. "The brooms will always sweep you out again, quick smart."

Elly looked behind her. Sure enough, the small cupboard she'd just fallen out of was filled with brooms. One of them was still pushing at her feet, as if trying to sweep her as far away as possible.

There was a mirror stuck inside the

cupboard, and Elly was relieved to see that at least her hair and clothes had now gone back to normal.

"Elinora, go back to your seat straight away," barked Madame.

Elly hurried back, glaring at the smirking Cruddleperrys as she passed them. She longed to turn their hair green, but she knew Madame would be furious if anything else happened. And besides, the chances of her spell actually working were very slim.

Saphie gave Elly a cheeky smile as she sat down. "Don't worry about the Cruddleperrys doing any more spells on you,' she whispered. "If they even try, they're in for a very big surprise!"

Even though everything was back to normal, Elly still felt cross and fidgety.

I was crazy to think I could help Jess, she thought. *I can't even stop the Cruddleperrys from putting me in the broom closet!*

"Please find the Wish Fulfilment section in the Fairy Code, everyone," said Madame Fernyfrond briskly.

Uh-oh! thought Elly.

Her copy of the Fairy Code was at home. Was she about to get in trouble *again*? Then she noticed that everyone had simply flipped out their wand screens.

"The Fairy Code is loaded onto your wand," explained Saphie, showing her the right button to press.

"Saphie," said Madame Fernyfrond, "please read the page entitled *The Three Golden Rules of Wish Fulfilment* to the class."

Saphie stood up and read the rules.

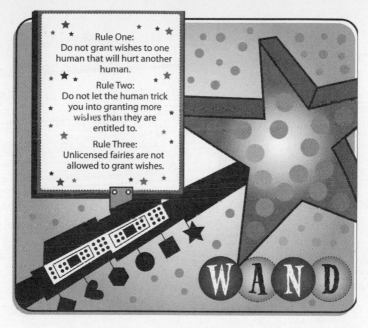

Rule One:
Do not grant wishes to one human that will hurt another human.

Rule Two:
Do not let the human trick you into granting more wishes than they are entitled to.

Rule Three:
Unlicensed fairies are not allowed to grant wishes.

WAND

"Thank you, Saphie," said Madame. "I want everyone to memorize those rules. Granting wishes to humans is the main task of fairies. Humans are annoying sometimes, but it is always our duty to help them out!"

Suddenly, all of Elly's doubts vanished, and she felt determined again.

I HAVE to help Jess! she told herself. *It's my duty as a fairy. And I'll find a way out of Rainbowville. I know I will!*

But how exactly was she going to do it?

Saphie will help me, thought Elly. But sneaking out of Rainbowville would be very risky. There was no way Elly wanted to get Saphie into trouble. *If she can just help me sneak out, I can do the rest,* Elly decided.

Elly put her wand into Cloud Writer mode. Then, when Madame's back was turned, she scribbled a message to Saphie, under the desk and well away from Cruddleperry eyes.

Can we talk at recess? Somewhere private.

Saphie smiled and nodded. *Of course!* she cloud-wrote back. *Let's go to the library.*

Chapter Eight

The moment the recess bell went, Elly and Saphie raced for the door.

"Going to play with all your friends in the library again, are you?" sneered Gabi.

Saphie shrugged. "Books are way more fun to hang out with than you Cruddleperrys," she said. "And they smell better too."

"You know, Gabi," said Nadia, pulling out her wand. "I've heard that humans often wish they could turn into animals."

"Really?" replied Gabi, grinning nastily. "Well, you should probably practise that spell, Nadia."

"I think that's a bad idea," said Saphie calmly. "It's against Academy rules."

"Oh, *really?*" laughed Nadia. "Well, we think it's a great idea."

Then she and Gabi pointed their wands at Elly and Saphie. There was a flash of light and a shower of purple stars!

Elly squeezed her eyes tightly shut. *What have they turned us into?* she wondered. *Probably something slimy.* Then Elly heard a scream. It sounded a bit like Gabi, but something wasn't quite right about it.

Elly opened her eyes, and gasped. Standing where the Cruddleperrys had been were two scaly green lizards!

84

"What have you done to us?" shrieked one of the lizards, who looked a bit like Nadia.

"You did it to yourselves," retorted Saphie. "I did warn you."

"But we can't stay like this," cried the other lizard, who looked a bit like Gabi. "You have to change us back!"

"I can't," replied Saphie. "It's very hard to reverse a spell you've done on yourself. You'll have to go to the school nurse."

"But we'll get in huge trouble if we do that!" wailed Gabi.

"Rule number 40," called the Ruler from inside Elly's backpack. "No unsupervised spells by unlicensed fairies!"

"You have to help us!" insisted the lizards, waving their tails around.

"Rule number 41," said the Ruler instantly. "No helping fairies who have broken rule number 40." Then the Ruler gave a funny little cough, like it was trying not to laugh.

"Sorry," said Elly. "We'd love to help, but you heard the Rule Ruler. Besides, we've got to hang out with our friends in the library." Then she grabbed Saphie's arm and they glided off down the corridor.

Once they were safely around the corner, both fairies stopped and laughed until their faces ached.

"How did you *do* that?" giggled Elly.

"Well," grinned Saphie, "while you cleverly distracted everyone by falling out of the broom closet, I snuck over and put their

wands in reverse. So any spells they tried to put on us would backfire onto them! I think they make much nicer lizards than fairies."

"*Definitely!*" laughed Elly, as she and Saphic headed off to the library.

The library was vast and echoey, with high walls completely covered in bookshelves. Even the window ledges were stacked so high with piles of books that it was almost impossible to see outside.

"No one but me reads these books anymore. The others all look at wandbooks instead," said Saphie, as she checked to make sure they were totally alone. "The saddest part is that if these books don't get read, they just crumble away to dust."

As Elly walked along, the books seemed to make a whispering, rustling sound.

"It's like they're asking me to read them," said Elly.

"They are," said Saphie. "Those are Tell Tale books—they're a record of all the naughty things Rainbow Academy students have done over the years. They're probably dying to tell you everything."

Then Elly spotted something glinting under one of the shelves. She bent down and fished it out. It was a tiny book, no bigger than her hand, with golden edges. It was very dusty and crumbly.

Poor old book, thought Elly. If someone didn't read it soon, it would probably vanish completely. Elly slipped the book into her backpack, giving it a reassuring pat as she

did. *Don't worry,* she told the book silently.
I'll read you.

"Now," said Saphie, once they were sure
no one was hiding anywhere, "what did you
want to talk about?"

So Elly explained all about Jess. She even
told Saphie her big secret—that Jess knew
Elly was a fairy! This was strictly against Fairy
Code rules. If anyone found out about it, Elly
would be in huge trouble. But Elly knew she
could trust Saphie with her secret.

When Elly had finished, Saphie nodded.

"That's why you were so upset when Grandma said that Jess was being crushed," she said.

"Exactly," replied Elly. "And that's why I have to sneak over to the other side of the rainbow. Jess might need my help!"

"But how are you planning to sneak out?" asked Saphie.

"Well, I thought *you* might have some ideas," said Elly hopefully.

But Saphie looked unsure. "It's pretty much impossible to sneak out of Rainbowville," she said. "The last time any unlicensed fairies left Rainbowville was ages ago. It used to be a fairy's job to scan the sky for fairies going in and out of Rainbowville. This particular time, the fairy on duty fell asleep, so two Rainbow Academy students snuck out. They both got into huge trouble when they were caught.

Then the automatic Sky Scanner was invented and no one has ever gotten past it."

"I guess it's hopeless then," Elly frowned. "Besides, it's not just the Sky Scanner. There's also the problem of sneaking out of the Rainbow Academy itself! This place is covered with fairy sensors."

"Well, actually," said Saphie, lowering her voice, "*that* bit would be easy." She went over to one of the windows and carefully removed the books stacked on the windowsill.

Elly held her breath. Usually when you touched one of the Academy windows they started beeping furiously, but this one remained silent. Saphie pushed on it, and with a gentle creak the window swung open.

"It's been broken for ages," explained Saphie, "but no one comes down here, so I'm the only one who knows about it."

Her eyes sparkling, Elly hugged her friend. "Thanks so much," she said gratefully. "You've just solved half of the problem."

Suddenly, Saphie sat up straight. "You know what?" she said slowly. "I found a book when I first arrived here that had fallen down the back of the shelves. I got the feeling it wasn't really meant to be there, in fact. I started reading it because it looked so neglected."

"What was it about?" asked Elly.

"The Sky Scanner," said Saphie. Then her voice dropped to a whisper. "It said that it's possible to switch it into maintenance mode."

Elly frowned. "Maintenance mode?"

Saphie nodded. She was starting to look excited. "Yes. If I understood correctly, it

would be like shutting it down for repairs. It'd only be temporary, of course. But while it was in that mode, it wouldn't be able to connect with the Cloud Writer."

Elly raised an eyebrow and grinned.

Saphie grinned back. "Which means that for a short while, you could enter or exit Rainbowville, and no one would have a clue."

Elly jumped up immediately. "Saphie! Where is the book?"

But Saphie looked embarrassed. "It was a really boring book," she admitted. "I actually fell asleep while reading it. When I woke up, it had completely turned to dust."

Elly slumped back down in her seat. It was terrible to come so close to forming a plan, only to have it slip away.

Saphie smiled. "But you know, I think

I'd remember what it said if I was actually looking at the Sky Scanner," she said. "The whole thing is going to be risky. Very risky. But let's go to the Rainbow Lab tonight and see if I can work out what to do."

Elly shook her head. "I don't want you getting into trouble, Saph," she said. "If you tell me what you remember, I'll do it on my own. And I'll go tonight."

Saphie looked horrified. "Are you kidding?" There's no way I'm letting you go on a big adventure like this without me!"

Elly felt her Heart Tracker pendant glow with warmth. She knew she should insist that Saphie stay behind, but it would be so nice to have her there.

"Thanks, Saph," said Elly gratefully. Then she thought of something. "Hang on. How are we going to get into the Rainbow Lab? It's behind a huge gate!"

But Saph smiled mysteriously. "I think I have an answer to that. But there's no time to explain right now. Come on, we'd better get back."

As they left the library, Elly felt a tingle of excitement. There was no doubt that a very big task lay ahead of them. But it would all be worth it if she managed to help Jess!

Chapter Nine

Neither of the Cruddleperrys were around when Elly and Saphie went to bed that night.

"Evie told me that they're both in the sick room, being changed back from lizards," said Saphie. "They tried to blame us, of course, but the nurse guessed straight away what had happened. I bet they're furious!"

"I'm so excited about tonight that I don't even care about the Cruddleperrys," said Elly, bouncing on her bed. "What should we take?"

"Maybe our Extreme Flying turbo boosters," suggested Saphie. "Just in case."

"OK," said Elly. "But I really hope I don't have to use them!"

Suddenly, Saphie's face fell. "Wait a minute, I just thought of a problem. A *big* one."

"What?" asked Elly nervously.

"We need a rainbow umbrella. Without that, we can't re-enter Rainbowville."

Elly pulled open her backpack and rummaged around. "Do you mean one of these, by any chance?" She smiled, pulling out Grandmother's rainbow umbrella. "I'd totally forgotten I even had it!"

Saphie laughed and shook her head. "You are amazing, Elly! Now, we better get some sleep. We've got a huge job ahead of us."

"I'll try," said Elly, as she climbed into bed fully dressed. "But I don't think it's likely. I'm way too excited."

But Elly must have fallen asleep, because the next thing she knew, Saphie was shaking her awake.

"Here," said Saphie, handing her what looked like a very long, flat cushion. "Put this in your bed and tuck the covers around it."

"What is it?" asked Elly curiously.

"It's a replacer balloon," said Saphie. "They make it look like you're still in your bed, when you're not. I got them in a fairy show

bag once. I knew they'd come in handy!"

Elly pushed her replacer balloon into her bed. Instantly, it inflated to her exact size and shape. When the covers were drawn up around it, Elly nearly laughed. It looked exactly like she was still in there!

If the Rule Ruler saw this, it would go totally crazy, she grinned to herself.

Luckily, the Ruler seemed to be asleep. Elly could hear little woody snores coming from her backpack as she slipped it on.

Elly and Saphie snuck out of the dormitory and headed toward the Rainbow Laboratory. The corridors of the Academy were bathed in the soft, silvery light of the full moon.

It was so quiet that it made Elly jumpy. She was glad when they finally arrived at the gates. She kept expecting someone to leap out of the shadows and catch them!

But when Elly looked properly at the gates, she frowned. "Uh, Saph?" she said. "Any ideas on how we get past these?"

Saphie gave her a grin. "Yes, actually. I found another interesting book in the library a while back," she said. Then she glanced at her watch, and whispered, "In exactly one minute, the full moon will have completely risen. Then, if the book was right, something pretty freaky will happen."

"What?" asked Elly, bursting with curiosity.

But Saphie shook her head. "Wait and see. You won't believe me if I tell you."

Suddenly, the corridor was aglow with bright beams of moonlight.

Saphie grabbed Elly's hand. "Come on!" she whispered urgently. "We have to walk

through the gates now, while the moon is at its brightest!"

Saphie started walking toward the gates, but Elly hesitated. "Saph, the gates are locked, remember?" she said, confused.

"You have to trust me," said Saphie softly. "I'll explain later."

So Elly walked quickly toward the gate.

She scrunched her eyes closed, waiting to crash into the metal bars. But no crash came.

"It worked!" chuckled Saphie.

Elly opened her eyes and discovered, to her amazement, that they were now standing on the other side of the gate, at the top of the stairs. "Hang on," she said. "What just happened?"

"The gate is made from *moon metal*," explained Saphie.

"What's that?" asked Elly.

"It's a fairy metal made from moonbeams," explained Saphie. "Usually it's super strong. But on very bright full-moon nights, it turns back into beams of light—even though it still looks totally solid!"

Elly wasn't sure that she believed Saphie. She reached out for the gate, but again her

hand went straight through it!

"That's amazing!" she marvelled. "It's so lucky you read that book, Saph."

"I read everything. Even boring old books about gates," laughed Saphie. "Come on. We'd better hurry!"

Elly and Saphie hurried down the narrow stairs into the darkness, toward the door of the Rainbow Lab. They didn't dare use a torch, in case someone walking past noticed the light. The further down the stairs they went, the darker things got. Elly was really glad that Saphie was there with her.

Gradually, Elly noticed a strange flickering light reflected on the walls. One moment it was red, then it was purple and then, almost as quickly, it changed to blue.

"I think that's the rainbow we can see!"

whispered Saphie excitedly. "It must be shining under the door of the Rainbow Lab."

The lights became brighter and brighter as Elly and Saphie went further down the stairs, until the narrow stairwell glowed with colour.

"I think we're near the entrance of the Rainbow Lab," said Saphie, her eyes wide.

Elly felt shivery with excitement. "I can't believe we're about to see where the rainbow actually comes from!" she said.

"Me neither!" said Saphie. Then suddenly, she stopped. "There's just one problem."

"What?" asked Elly.

Saphie pointed. "That," she said. Up ahead was a very solid-looking door.

Chapter Ten

Elly put out her hand and grasped the small, golden handle on the door. *Please don't be locked!* she pleaded silently.

Then she turned the handle and, to her delight, the door swung open with a creak.

"I don't believe it!" laughed Saphie.

"Maybe I'm better at magic than you realize," grinned Elly.

"Maybe you're just lucky!" laughed Saphie.

Then they both crept into the Rainbow Laboratory. The lab was very small. Its curved walls and ceiling were painted a deep blue, with shining stars sprinkled across it.

"It's so weird to think that we're actually under the ground," said Saphie.

"I know!" agreed Elly. "All these stars make me feel like I'm floating in the sky."

Near the door was what looked like a very high-tech golden telescope, poking out through the roof of the Laboratory.

"That must be the Sky Scanner," said Saphie. Then she grabbed Elly's arm and pointed. "Look!"

Elly looked where Saphie was pointing. In the middle of the room was a very simple, old-fashioned spinning wheel. Threaded across it was a length of material so fine and

silky that it was almost transparent.

The fabric stretched up to the roof of the Laboratory and disappeared into a golden pipe in the centre of the ceiling. A fine mist of tiny multi-coloured raindrops hovered around the spinning wheel, sparkling and twinkling like a scattering of jewels.

"The rainbow," breathed Elly.

"I can't believe we're actually looking at it *being made!*" said Saphie.

Elly longed to touch the beautiful fabric spinning around the wheel. It contained every colour Elly had ever seen, and some extra ones too.

She had felt the rainbow, of course, when she slid over it into Rainbowville. But this new material looked different somehow. Elly's hand crept toward the spinning wheel,

 108

almost as if it had a mind of its own.

"Elinora Knottleweed-Eversprightly!" said Saphie suddenly. "Stay away from that! The rainbow is very delicate when it's freshly spun. It's not until it reaches the outside air that it becomes hard enough to touch."

Elly laughed guiltily. "You sounded like my grandmother then," she said.

"Sometimes I know just how she feels, having to keep an eye on you all the time!" grinned Saphie.

Saphie flipped open a panel on the Sky Scanner. Inside was a criss-crossing tumble of silver wires and flashing, beeping buttons. Saphie's face fell. "Uh-oh," she said. "This is going to be more complicated than I thought. I'll probably need to re-do all this wiring. It's going to take a while to figure it out."

"Can I help?" asked Elly.

Saphie smiled. "Thanks, Elly," she said. "But it'll probably be better if I try to sort it out myself."

Elly knew what Saphie meant. It wasn't that Elly tried to cause disasters. They just seemed to find her, wherever she went!

Elly wandered over to the middle of the room and watched the rainbow spinner again. *I really want to touch that rainbow fabric,* thought Elly longingly. She glanced at Saphie. She was busily working on the Sky Scanner.

I'm sure it'll be OK, if I'm very careful, decided Elly. Then she reached out her hand and gently touched the newly spun rainbow.

The rainbow was very sticky. So sticky, in fact, that it instantly stuck to Elly's fingers! Elly quickly pulled her hand away, trying not

to rip the delicate fabric. With a thumping heart, she examined the multi-coloured fabric before it disappeared up through the pipe in the roof. Part of the red threads had become stuck to the orange threads.

I didn't make a hole in it, at least, thought Elly, relieved. She shot a glance at Saphie, who was hunched over the Sky Scanner. Elly couldn't help feeling very glad her friend didn't know what she'd done!

I'd better move away from the rainbow so I don't touch it again, decided Elly.

She hurried back over to where Saphie was still puzzling over the Sky Scanner controls. "How's it going?" she asked.

Saphie sat up and wiped some grease from her nose. "Not so well," she admitted. "I can't work out which wires I need to swap. I wish I

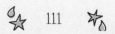

hadn't fallen asleep while reading that book."

Elly looked over Saphie's shoulder, feeling worried. If Saphie couldn't work this out, the whole mission would have to be called off. Then suddenly, she noticed a big red button. On it was written *Maintenance Mode*.

"What does that button do?" Elly asked, pointing at it.

Saphie looked up. Then she burst out laughing. "I didn't notice that!" she said. "I've been wasting all this time worrying about

wires when we can just push the button."

"You would've noticed it in the end," said Elly kindly.

Saphie put her arm around Elly's shoulder. "You know, you really are an excellent fairy," she said. "OK, so you have the occasional accident. But you always figure things out in the end. And you often do it in a much better way than anyone else."

Elly went red. She was so used to being told how hopeless she was that it was kind of embarrassing to be told the opposite.

Saphie might not think I was such a great fairy if she'd seen what almost happened to the rainbow, thought Elly guiltily.

Saphie pressed the button. Straight away, the Sky Scanner made a strange squealing sound, like a car screeching to a stop.

"We've done it!" said Saphie excitedly. "It's in Maintenance Mode. But we've only got an hour to visit Jess and get back again, before the Sky Scanner turns back on automatically. We should be OK once we get over the rainbow, because of the time difference. But if we're not back here in time, our names will be written across the sky in red."

Elly raced for the Laboratory door. "Well, come on then," she called over her shoulder. "Let's get going!"

Elly and Saphie padded back up the dark stairwell as fast as they could, and pushed back through the moon-metal gate just as the bright moonlight began to fade. Then they glided back through the empty corridors toward the library.

As they zoomed past the sick room, Elly's

heart skipped a beat. She could've sworn she saw a small, dark shape scurry behind the door. But when she looked again, the shape wasn't there.

Stop imagining things! she told herself severely. *Everyone is fast asleep!*

Still, Elly was very glad when they finally reached the library door and snuck inside.

Straight away, Saphie rushed to the broken window and started clearing the books from the window sill. Usually Saphie was very careful with books. But Elly could see that tonight she was hurrying.

A big, heavy book fell to the ground with a clatter. Elly and Saphie both froze. Had anyone heard?

"Get ready to hide!" muttered Saphie. But no one appeared. Elly sighed with relief, then

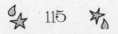

hurried over to the broken window.

"Quick! Put on your turbo boosters!" whispered Saphie.

"Umm, are you sure that's a good idea?" Elly muttered back. "I didn't have a lot of success with them last time. Remember that whole zooming around upside down episode?"

Saphie smiled. "This time will be different," she said reassuringly, climbing up onto the window ledge and preparing for flight. "I'll be right beside you!"

Chapter Eleven

If you'd been walking through a certain park in a certain town on a certain night quite recently, you would've seen something *very* unusual. Firstly, a rainbow appeared from nowhere, reaching down from the sky until it touched the path beside the fountain.

Then, a moment later, two small figures came whooshing at high-speed down the rainbow. They both landed lightly on the ground, then took off like rockets into the darkness. Seconds later, the rainbow vanished.

But you weren't around that particular night, so you didn't see anything. In fact, no one did. Everyone was already tucked up safely in bed. If you'd listened carefully though, you might've heard some giggling. This was coming from Elly. She was laughing even though she had loads of things to worry about that night. The reason she was laughing was because, for the first time ever, she was actually enjoying flying!

Saphie, it turned out, was an excellent Extreme Flying teacher. First, she'd shown Elly how to hold her arms out to stop herself tipping sideways. Then, she'd shown Elly how holding one foot slightly higher than the other prevents her from rolling.

Finally, she'd taught Elly a simple trick—
if you take big, deep breaths, you stay high!

"So what do you think of Extreme Flying
now?" called Saphie as Elly zoomed past her.

"Well, I never thought I'd say this,"
called Elly, "but this is *almost* as fun as
skateboarding!"

"See!" grinned Saphie. "I knew you'd like
it once you got the hang of it."

Then Elly gave a shout. "That's Jess's
house down there!"

All of a sudden, there were butterflies in
Elly's stomach. *What if Jess is really hurt?* she
worried. *What if I'm too late?*

Elly and Saphie flew down and landed in the Chesters' backyard, behind the pottery studio.

"You go and see Jess," whispered Saphie. "I'll keep watch."

Elly hesitated. *Jess and Saphie would get along really well,* she thought.

But unlicensed fairies aren't supposed to meet humans, and Saphie had already taken enough risks to help her out. It would be better if she just kept watch.

"OK, thanks, Saphie," said Elly, giving her friend a hug.

It was strange being back in her old street. Elly felt a pang of sadness when she saw her own house, looking so dark and empty. *I wonder how long it will be before I'm back there with my family?*

But there was no time to think about that. She had to concentrate on helping Jess!

Elly crept around to Jess's bedroom window and peeked in through a crack in the blinds. She could see Jess, sound asleep in her bed. On her bedside table was the Hoverlamp that Elly had given Jess when she left South Street School. It was glowing faintly.

Jess doesn't look crushed, thought Elly, relieved. *But it's hard to tell. Maybe the squashed bits are under the covers?*

Elly tapped on the window. At first, Jess didn't move. So Elly tapped louder, and then Jess sat up with a start.

"Jess! Over here!" hissed Elly.

Jess caught sight of her. Grinning broadly, she leapt over and flung open the window.

"Wow! It's so great to see you!" she said,

as she helped Elly inside. "I've missed you so much!"

"I've missed you heaps too," said Elly. Then she remembered why she was there. "Are you OK?" she asked urgently. "The Human Database said you were hurt."

Jess looked surprised. "I'm fine," she said.

"Are you sure?" asked Elly. "The Database said you'd been crushed."

Suddenly, Jess's face went bright red. "Oh," she said. "I think I know what's going on. How embarrassing!"

"What?" asked Elly. She still didn't know whether to feel relieved or worried.

Jess sat down on the side of the bed, her face getting pinker by the second. The Hoverlamp flew up from the bedside table and landed in her lap, its motor whirring.

"I'm afraid you've come all this way for nothing," said Jess apologetically. "You see, I haven't *been* crushed. I *have* a crush. Just a tiny little one, on someone at school. I can't believe it's in your Database! I haven't told anyone."

Elly was so glad that Jess was OK that she wanted to laugh. But she had a feeling this might make Jess even more embarrassed.

"Who do you have the crush on?" she asked curiously.

"His name is Josh," said Jess with a sigh. "He started at South Street School just after you left. He's funny and smart and he's got brown hair and smiley brown eyes."

"Why are you sighing then, if he's so nice?" asked Elly.

"He doesn't even know I exist!" said Jess sadly. "I think he likes Caitlin more than me. She's so perfect."

Elly put her arm around Jess. "You are the most totally awesome human ever," she said. "If Josh doesn't like you he must be crazy."

Then the Hoverlamp flew up in the air and did three mad loops of the room.

"See, the Hoverlamp agrees with me," laughed Elly.

Jess gave a small smile. "You know, for the first time ever I almost wish you could do some magic," she said. "I would so love to know if Josh likes me."

Elly had never seen her friend like this before. Usually the last thing Jess wanted was for Elly to do magic! Jess didn't seem herself at all. In fact, she seemed kind of flat.

Having a crush must be a bit like being crushed after all, decided Elly. She really wanted to help her friend, but she didn't know any spells that would help Jess. And even if she did, it was against the Fairy Code for an unlicensed fairy to grant wishes.

Then suddenly, she felt a warm sensation on her chest. It was her Heart Tracker pendant, glowing brightly.

Jess looked at it curiously. "That's so beautiful," she said, leaning over to look at it more closely. The closer she got, the more the pendant glowed.

Elly hesitated. The pendant made her feel less homesick. *But Jess could really use it,* thought Elly.

Quickly, she undid the clasp and handed the pendant to Jess. "Here," she said. "I want you to have it. Wear it when Josh is near. If it glows, it means he likes you. And if it doesn't glow, it means he's crazy!"

Jess looked at the necklace. For a moment, Elly thought she was going to refuse to take it. Then Jess slipped it around her neck and smiled gratefully. "Thanks, Elly," she said. "Hey, when are you and your family moving back home?"

126

Elly shrugged. "My family will have to come home first," she said.

"They will," said Jess confidently.

Just then, there was another tap on the window. "I should go," said Elly, jumping up.

"Thanks so much for the necklace," said Jess, hugging Elly goodbye. "You're the best fairy I've ever met."

"Hang on," laughed Elly. "I'm the *only* fairy you've ever met!"

But all the same, Elly felt good. Giving away her special pendant was worth it if it helped Jess.

chapter Twelve

Elly slipped out of Jess's window to find Saphie already hovering in mid-air.

"Is everything OK?" Saphie asked.

"She's going to be just fine," said Elly, smiling. "We'd better get flying!"

Now that she'd gotten the hang of Extreme Flying, she was actually looking forward to zooming back at top speed.

Side by side, Elly and Saphie flew as quickly as they could back to the park. After

they'd landed near the fountain, Elly pulled Grandmother's rainbow umbrella out of her backpack. The moment she'd opened it, a rainbow slowly began to form.

When it was ready, Elly and Saphie climbed on and soon they were zooming up and over the multi-coloured arch. The turbo boosters made the ride extremely fast!

Let's just hope the Sky Scanner is still out of action! thought Elly, as they crossed into Rainbowville. The Cloud Writer floated past and Elly held her breath.

A wiggle of cloud formed near the tip of the Cloud Writer.

Uh oh! thought Elly. *It's about to write something!* But to her relief, no letters appeared.

With a *whoosh*, the two fairies slid down the last stretch of rainbow and landed with a gentle thud in the golden pot. Together, they zoomed through the air back to the Academy.

They squeezed back through the broken library window, and collapsed, exhausted, against the library shelves.

"I can't believe we actually did it!" laughed Saphie. "We've been in and out of Rainbowville, and no one caught us."

"I wonder what our grandmothers would say if they knew?" giggled Elly.

Then she nearly jumped out of her skin when a voice said from the darkness, "Well,

why don't you ask them?"

A light snapped on. There, in front of Elly and Saphie, were Madame Fernyfrond and Grandmother Knottleweed-Eversprightly.

And beside them stood Gabi and Nadia, who had been changed back into fairies. But they still looked a lot like lizards. Their skin was still greenish and scaly, and they both had long tails sticking out below their dressing gowns!

Usually this would've made Elly laugh. But one look at the faces of Madame Fernyfrond and Grandmother Knottleweed-Eversprightly warned her that laughing probably wasn't a good idea.

"I think we might be in a bit of trouble!" she muttered to Saphie.

"I can't believe you would behave so

badly," said Madame Fernyfrond to Saphie, shaking her head. "What were you thinking?"

"Clearly they weren't thinking at all, Emerelda," snapped Grandmother. "They have behaved like, well, like *humans!*"

Then, as if being told off by the grandmothers wasn't enough, the Ruler in Elly's backpack finally woke up and decided to make up for lost time.

"Rule number 798!" the Ruler called. "No behaving like humans! Rule number 18! No sneaking out of Rainbowville!"

"It's just lucky Gabi saw you leaving, and alerted us to what was going on," said Madame Fernyfrond.

That must have been the dark shape I saw when we flew past the sick room, realized Elly. *I should've guessed it was a Cruddleperry!*

"When Madame Fernyfrond called to tell me what you'd done, I was shocked. *Shocked!*" said Grandmother to Elly. "Sneaking out of Rainbowville is bad enough. But trying to ruin the rainbow is absolutely unforgivable!"

Elly stared at her grandmother, confused. "I didn't ruin anything!"

"Don't pretend you weren't responsible for that, Elinora," snapped Grandmother, pointing out the window. Outside, dawn was just beginning to break beneath the rainbow.

Except, as Elly realized with horror, it wasn't actually a rain*bow* anymore. It was a rain-*knot!*

Instead of forming a perfect arch, the colours were all tangled around each other. It was a huge, ugly mess.

"We didn't do that!" insisted Saphie.

RAIN-KNOT

"Well, actually," said Elly, in a small voice, "it might've been my fault. I touched it."

"Oh, Elly," said Saphie, shaking her head. She looked like she didn't know whether to laugh or cry.

"Don't you know that even the *slightest* disturbance to the freshly spun rainbow fabric can *completely* alter the form and shape the rainbow takes?" demanded Grandmother.

"It will take a lot of hard work to get the

rainbow back to its proper shape," frowned Madame Fernyfrond. "We're just fortunate that this half of the rainbow isn't visible to the humans on the other side. Imagine the confusion a rain-knot would cause the humans!"

"Rule number 124," added the Ruler. "No messing up the rainbow!"

Elly wished she could disappear into the floor. It felt like everyone was angry with her. Before she knew it, she'd burst into tears.

"I'm sorry!" she wailed. "I just wanted to see if Jess was OK."

Grandmother frowned at Elly. "And who, precisely, is *Jess*?" she asked sternly.

But before Elly could answer, her backpack slid off. And as it fell, the Tell Tale book Elly had shoved in it earlier tumbled out, flipping open when it hit the ground.

The book coughed a couple of times, as if to clear away the dust. Then it began speaking in a loud, clear voice. "Fifibella Knottleweed-Eversprightly," it said, "snuck out of the Rainbow Academy with her friend Emerelda Fernyfrond. Both fairies then left Rainbowville without permission, and stayed outside for an entire human day—eating human candies!"

Quickly, Elly slammed the book shut. But it was too late. Madame's mouth dropped open in astonishment. Grandmother Knottleweed-Eversprightly's face became very pale. For a moment, no one said anything.

Then to Elly's astonishment, Madame Fernyfrond started to chuckle. It started as a low, deep rumble that seemed to work its way

up her chest until it exploded into the air.

"Do you remember that day, Fifi?" chuckled Madame Fernyfrond. "Do you remember how we had to tiptoe around the Sky Scanner Fairy, and she was snoring so *loudly*?"

Grandmother Knottleweed-Eversprightly frowned and opened her mouth to speak. Then something very strange happened to her face. The corners of her mouth began twitching. Then her eyes started crinkling up.

And then a very peculiar noise poured out of her mouth. Grandmother was laughing! And once Grandmother started laughing, she couldn't seem to stop.

"I can still picture everyone's faces when they caught us sneaking back in. I've never been more terrified!" she chortled.

"Our headfairy put us on dish-washing

duty for three months straight!" laughed Madame Fernyfrond. "And she confiscated our wands for the rest of the year!"

Elly, Saphie, Gabi and Nadia looked at each other in confusion. They had never seen adult fairies behave like this before.

Finally, Grandmother wiped a tear away from the corner of her eye. "Elly," she said, "I've never told you this, but when I was your

age I was *always* getting into trouble."

"Really?" said Elly. It was hard to even imagine Grandmother being her age, let alone getting into trouble!

"I'm afraid it's true," smiled Madame Fernyfrond. "We were *both* very badly behaved. In fact, your grandmother had been to a number of other schools before she came to the Rainbow Academy. And she very nearly got expelled from here too!"

Grandmother was a fairy school drop-out, just like me! thought Elly, amazed.

"But after the rainbow incident I became much better behaved. I even topped my class in my final year!" said Grandmother proudly.

"You did very well, Fifi," said Madame Fernyfrond softly. "But perhaps Elly is just not cut out for fairy life? Perhaps it's time to start considering other options."

"You mean . . ." said Grandmother.

Madame Fernyfrond nodded. "Yes. Maybe Elly should stop trying to be a fairy, and start living like a human."

Everyone turned and looked at Elly.

"Is that what you'd like to do?" asked Grandmother, in a surprisingly gentle voice. "Would you like to stop being a fairy forever?"

"Um, well, but I . . ." Elly started to say. Then she stopped. She could feel a warmth in her chest. It was the same feeling that the Heart Tracker pendant used to create.

But Jess had the pendant. *What's going on?* Elly wondered.

Chapter Thirteen

There was a knock on the library door, and then a familiar voice called out, "Hello? Is anyone there?"

Then the door was flung open and a small, dribbly figure flew at Elly and flung its arms around her.

"Kara!" laughed Elly, hugging her little sister. Then Elly's parents stepped into the room too, and the warm feeling in Elly's chest grew stronger and stronger.

I didn't need the Heart Tracker at all! thought Elly happily. *I knew they were here anyway.*

"It is so good to see you," said Elly's mum, hugging her tightly. "We missed you so much!"

"We would've been here sooner," added Elly's dad, "but we had trouble getting across the rainbow. It seems to be malfunctioning."

Suddenly, everyone was staring at Elly again.

"Before your arrival, we'd just asked Elinora a very important question," explained Grandmother to Elly's parents. "We haven't heard her answer yet."

"Yeah, Elly," sneered Gabi. "What are you going to do? Are you going to give up your wand and live like a human?"

"Or are you going to keep being a terrible

fairy?" sniggered Nadia.

"I think it's about time that you two went back to the sick room," snapped Madame Fernyfrond. "And don't think that just because you alerted me to Elly and Saphie's escape, you can avoid punishment. You broke the school rules today by performing a serious spell without supervision. You are on pest control for the rest of the year."

"I suspect they'll be keeping those scaly skins for some time," said Grandmother, eyeing the two lizardy fairies. "That should make them think twice about breaking important Academy rules again."

Gabi and Nadia looked very cross, but they turned and stalked out of the library.

Then Elly's mum looked at her very seriously. "Maybe it *would* be best if you gave up your wings, darling," she said.

"You could go back to South Street School and be just like all the human children," added her dad.

Elly looked around. It felt like everyone had already decided that she should give up being a fairy. It was weird. She *had* thought that she'd be much better suited to living like a human. But now that she was being offered the chance to change, she suddenly wasn't so sure she wanted it.

It's true that I'm not the best at doing spells, thought Elly, *but I've still managed to grant wishes for Jess.* Granting wishes felt good. It felt like something she was *meant* to do. Would she still be able to grant wishes if she gave up being a fairy?

I always thought that skateboarding was way

more fun than flying. Elly frowned to herself. *But flying along with Saphie tonight was pretty cool. It'd be a shame to give up flying just as I'm getting the hang of it.*

Then she looked at Saphie. *I probably couldn't stay friends with Saph if I stop being a fairy, either.*

"Well, Elinora?" said Grandmother. "Have you made your decision?"

Elly nodded. "Yes," she said. "I've decided that I want to keep being a fairy."

For a moment, everyone seemed too surprised to say anything.

Then Saphie threw her arms around her. "I'm so glad to hear that!" she said.

"Are you sure?" asked Elly's mum. "I thought you hated being a fairy!"

Elly shrugged. "I thought I did too. But you know, I actually *want* to be a fairy now."

"Well that is just splendid news!" said Grandmother, beaming. Elly had never seen her look so happy.

"But," added Elly quickly, "I'll probably always do things a little differently than all the other fairies. And I'll probably keep making mistakes. It's just the way I am."

Grandmother frowned, but before she

could speak, Saphie jumped in. "It's good that you do things differently, Elly," she said. "Who knows—maybe you can teach the rest of us some things!"

"What about school?" asked Elly's dad. "You should really go to a fairy school if you want to keep training as a fairy."

"Well, actually," said Elly, "if it's OK with Madame Fernyfrond, I'd like to stay here at the Rainbow Academy. I get the feeling that I could learn lots of useful things here. Besides," she laughed, "I can't wait to see what food we get on pink day!"

"I don't know," said Elly's mother, looking worried. "We really missed you while we were away, and the house would be so empty if you stayed here as a boarder."

Kara clung on tightly to Elly's neck, and

did an extra-specially big dribble to show that she agreed.

"Elly could come to the Rainbow Academy as a day student!" suggested Saphie. "Couldn't she catch the Fairy Flock into Rainbowville everyday?"

Then Saphie turned to Madame and added, a little shyly, "Grandma, I miss my parents too. Maybe Elly and I could be day students together?"

Elly's heart leapt. The Fairy Flock was the

way most unlicensed fairies got to school, travelling in one big group disguised as a cloud. Usually, Elly hated it. *But I could get used to the Fairy Flock,* she grinned to herself, *if it meant I could see Saphie* and *Jess everyday!*

Now everyone's attention turned to Madame Fernyfrond.

"What do you think, Emmy?" asked Grandmother, raising an eyebrow. "Are you prepared to keep my granddaughter on at your school as a day student?"

"Of course!" replied Madame Fernyfrond promptly. "I never had any doubts about that."

Elly grinned. "Thanks so much, Madame Fernyfrond," she said earnestly. "I promise I won't let you down."

"And Sapphire, you and I will need to

talk to your parents," Madame said. Then she suddenly looked very serious. "But, there is one condition, Elinora. An important one."

"What is that, Madame?" asked Elly nervously. "I'll do anything I can."

"You and Sapphire must untangle the rainbow," said Madame. "There are about 2642 threads in the rainbow and you will need to straighten up every single one."

That would be like unravelling the biggest wool blanket in the whole world, and then putting it back together! Elly stared at Saphie and gulped. "Two thousand six hundred and foty-two threads?" she repeated. "That will take forever!"

"Not forever. But definitely every spare moment for the rest of the week," smiled Madame Fernyfrond. "It will be a fiddly job,

and very, very boring. Are you prepared to do it?"

"We'd love to, wouldn't we, Elly?" replied Saphie, linking her arm through Elly's.

Elly nodded. "Yes, Madame Fernyfrond," she said. "It'll be fun."

Then Elly's eyes fell on something near the door. It looked like her parents had brought her bag of treasured possessions from home—including her skateboard!

Maybe this untangling job really will be fun, she giggled to herself. *At least I'll have Saphie for company!*

Just then, a bell sounded.

"It's breakfast time, fairies!" said Madame Fernyfrond.

"Let's go and eat, Saph," said Elly. "I'm starving!"

Elly hugged her family one more time, then headed out the door, grabbing her skateboard and tucking it under her arm as she went.

As Elly closed the library door behind her, she heard Madame Fernyfrond say to the others, "You know, I have a feeling that young Elinora is going to make the Rainbow Academy proud one day. I think she has the makings of a very fine fairy indeed."

"As much as I hate to admit it," said Grandmother, sounding as if she couldn't quite believe what she was saying, "I think you might be right!"

It was lucky that Madame Fernyfrond and Grandmother didn't see what happened the moment Elly was outside the room. If they had, they might not have been quite so happy. For as soon as Elly was safely out of earshot, she put her skateboard down on the ground and hopped on.

"Come on!" she whispered excitedly to Saphie. "Climb on board. I've been dying to try my skateboard out on these super-slippery floors!"

Then she and Saphie whooshed off down the corridor.

Read more about Elly

in the first two books — **Fairy School Drop-out**

and **Fairy School Drop-out Undercover!**